Millie Marotta's
Animal Kingdom
Book of Prints

BATSFORD

First published in the United Kingdom in 2016 by
Batsford
1 Gower Street
London
WC1E 6HD

An imprint of Pavilion Books Group Ltd

ISBN: 9781849944014
A CIP catalogue record for this book is available
from the British Library.

20 19 18 17 16 15 16

10 9 8 7 6 5 4 3 2 1

Repro by Mission, Hong Kong
Printed by Toppan Leefung Printing Ltd, China

This book can be ordered direct from the publisher at the website:
www.pavilionbooks.com, or try your local bookshop.

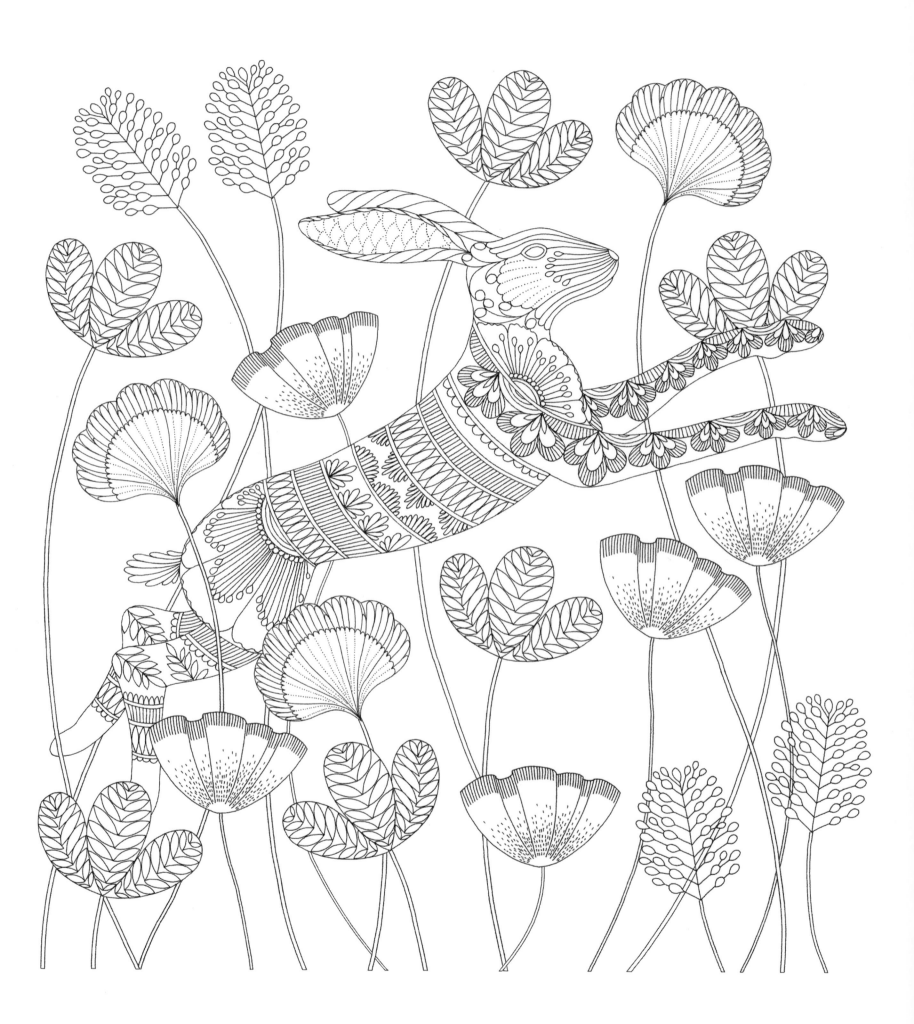